Weekly Reader Books Presents

GOOD HUNTING, BLUE SKY

by **Peggy Parish**
pictures by **James Watts**

An I Can Read Book®

Harper & Row, Publishers

For Kali, Megan and
Clarie Morris
and
For Tara and Justin Munn

This book is a presentation of Weekly Reader Books. Weekly Reader
Books offers book clubs for children from preschool through high school.
For further information write to: **Weekly Reader Books,**
4343 Equity Drive, Columbus, Ohio 43228.

Published by arrangement with Harper & Row, Publishers, Inc.
Weekly Reader is a federally registered trademark of Field
Publications. I Can Read Book is a registered trademark of
Harper & Row, Publishers, Inc.

Previously published by Addison-Wesley Publishing Company, Inc.,
under the title *Good Hunting, Little Indian.* The text has been
substantially revised for this edition.

Library of Congress Cataloging-in-Publication Data
Parish, Peggy.
  Good hunting, Blue Sky / by Peggy Parish ;
illustrated by James Watts. — New ed.
      p.   cm. — (An I can read book)
  Summary: Blue Sky, a young Indian boy, goes
hunting to bring food home only to have the food
bring him home instead.
  ISBN 0-06-024661-8 : $
  ISBN 0-06-024662-6 (lib. bdg.) : $
  [1. Indians of North America—Fiction.   2. Hunting
—Fiction.   3. Humorous stories.]   I. Watts,
James, 1955–   ill. II. Title. III. Series.
PZ7.P219Gm 1988   84-43143
[E]—dc19   CIP
                                                      AC

10   9   8   7   6   5   4   3   2   1
New Edition

"Look, Mama! Look, Papa!

Look what I made!"

said Blue Sky.

5

"A new bow?" asked Mama.

"Six new arrows!" said Blue Sky.

"You are so clever," said Mama.

"Are you going hunting?"
asked Papa.

"Yes," said Blue Sky.

"Today
I will bring home the meat."

"Good hunting, Blue Sky,"
said Mama.

"Bring home something big,"

said Papa.

"I will do my best,"

said Blue Sky.

Blue Sky walked quietly
into the forest.

Not a twig crackled.

Not a leaf crunched.

Blue Sky wanted to be

a good hunter,

and a good hunter

makes no noise.

11

Gobble, Gobble, Gobble.

Blue Sky stopped.

He listened.

Gobble, Gobble, Gobble.

Blue Sky looked up.

There sat a big turkey!

"Roasted turkey!" said Blue Sky.

"Mmmm, I like that."

He took an arrow

and aimed it

at the turkey.

He pulled the string back.

Away flew the arrow,

and...

away flew the turkey.

"Oh, well," said Blue Sky.

"That turkey was not very big.

I will find something bigger."

Blue Sky walked deeper

into the forest.

He looked all around.

Crackle, Crack, Crackle.

Quietly, quietly

Blue Sky crept

toward the noise.

Carefully he parted the bushes.

19

"Aha," said Blue Sky.

"A deer is bigger

than a turkey.

I will be very fast

with my bow and arrow."

And he was!

But the deer was faster.

He darted away

through the trees.

"That deer was bigger

than the turkey,"

said Blue Sky,

"but I will find something

even bigger."

Blue Sky looked for his arrow.

He found it in some bushes.

And he found something else.

Tracks! Animal tracks!

"Something *very* big

made those tracks,"

said Blue Sky.

"I wonder what it is."

Blue Sky turned around.

There stood a great big bear!

26

"Oh, no!" cried Blue Sky.

"You are *too* big."

Blue Sky scooted

to the top

of a tall tree.

"Please go away,"

he told the bear.

"I will not come down

until you go away."

The big bear sniffed

all around the tree.

He grunted loudly.

Then the big bear went away.

Blue Sky watched him go.

Then Blue Sky climbed down

from the tree.

He looked all around,

but he saw no animals.

Blue Sky stood very still

and listened,

but he heard no animals.

33

"I am not a good hunter,"

said Blue Sky.

34

"I might as well go home."

Blue Sky started back

toward the village.

Suddenly he heard—

CRASH CRACKLE CRASH.

The noise was

all around him.

Louder and louder,

closer and closer,

came the crashing noise.

"That has to be something big,"

said Blue Sky.

Suddenly—*WHOOSH!*—

out of the bushes

charged a ferocious wild boar!

38

Blue Sky knew what to do—

RUN!

He ran as fast as he could.

But the wild boar ran faster.

Blue Sky could see the village.

The boar was right behind him.

"Think quickly, Blue Sky,

think quickly!"

Blue Sky jumped high into the air.

He came down onto the boar's back.

The boar did not like this.

He ran faster.

He tried to dump Blue Sky.

Blue Sky grabbed the boar's ears.

He held on tight!

The boar raced into the village.

"Help! Help!" shouted Blue Sky.

"Papa, h-e-l-p!"

Papa saw the boar.

He saw Blue Sky.

Papa aimed his arrow at the boar—

WHIZZ.

Down went the boar.

Off went Blue Sky.

"Mama, come quickly!"

Papa called.

Mama came running.

She saw the boar.

"What a good hunter you are, Blue Sky,"

she said.

Blue Sky made a big fire.

Mama got the meat ready

to roast.

Papa called
all the people
in the village.

They all waited.

At last the meat was cooked.

What a feast they had!

Everybody ate

and ate

and ate.

Blue Sky told them
all about the hunt.

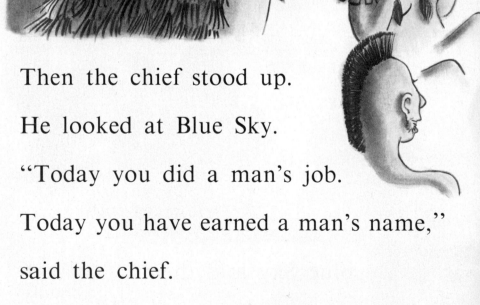

Then the chief stood up.

He looked at Blue Sky.

"Today you did a man's job.

Today you have earned a man's name,"

said the chief.

"Hear! Hear!" yelled the people.

"From this day on," said the chief,

"you will be called Big Hunter."

"Hurray for Big Hunter!"

yelled the people.

"But please, Big Hunter,"
said Papa,
"the next time you hunt,
you bring home the meat.
Don't let the meat
bring you home."